This book is dedicated to
Tyrone, Tahir and Niara.
Thank you for making this possible.
I love you.

www.tutusgreenworld.com

Copyright © 2011 by Tulani Thomas

Published by TuTu's Green World LLC
South Orange, NJ 07079

Illustrations by Seitu Hayden

♻ Printed on recycled paper

ISBN: 978-0-9846012-0-2

CPSIA Compliance Information: Batch 0511
For further information contact
RJ Communications
Phone 800 621-2556

Printed in the USA

TuTu Goes Green

Written by
Tulani Thomas

illustrated by
Seitu Hayden

TuTu cares about many things. She cares about her family and her friends. TuTu also cares about the earth. That is why TuTu lives a green life. She wants to take care of the earth.

Recycle

TuTu does many things to live green.
TuTu loves to recycle.
To recycle is to take something
that has been used before
and make it into something else.

TuTu recycles all of her old notebooks. She puts them in the bins at her school.

When the bins are full, all of the old notebooks are taken and made into new ones. Notebooks are made from trees, so TuTu is saving trees.

ReuSe

TuTu also loves to reuse old things.

To reuse is to use something
over and over again.

TuTu and her mother always reuse the same tote bags when they go to the market.

TuTu reuses old soup cans too.
She draws pretty pictures
on paper and glues the pictures
onto the cans.

She uses the decorated cans
to hold her pencils and markers.

TuTu reuses her favorite water bottle to drink water, juice, and milk.

Her mother washes it every day, so that TuTu can use it again and again.

Reduce

TuTu also reduces waste by
not using more than she needs.
She only uses things when
she needs them.

TuTu always turns off
the lights when she leaves
her room.

Her light bulbs are
a squiggly shape.
They save energy.

TuTu reduces waste by turning off the water when she brushes her teeth.

TuTu fills a cup with water to rinse her mouth. She does not want to waste a drop!

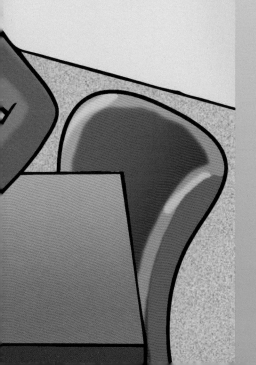

TuTu and her family like
to do many other things that
are good for the earth, too.

TuTu's mother cleans her room
with safe cleaners. They don't
have a harmful smell.
Her room smells fresh.

TuTu loves her soft bed.
Her pillows, sheets, and
blankets are made of a
special kind of cotton,
called organic.

Organic means that no
harmful chemicals were
used to grow the cotton.

TuTu always sleeps well
in her soft bed.

TuTu and her friends help
her father plant a tree
in the garden.

Trees help to clean the air.
TuTu and her friends will sit
under the tree when
it grows big and tall.

TuTu loves living green,
because it keeps our world clean!

The End